GOBI DESERT

HEILONGJIANG

INNER MONGOLIA
AUTONOMOUS REGION

JILIN

LIAONING

NORTH
KOREA

Sea of
Japan
(East Sea)

JAPAN

NINGXIA HUI
AUTONOMOUS
REGION

BEIJING
◉ BEIJING

Tianjin ●
TIANJIN

Bohai
Sea

SOUTH
KOREA

HEBEI

SHANXI

SHANDONG

Yellow
Sea

River

SHAANXI

Yellow

Xi'an ●

HENAN

JIANGSU

ANHUI

Nanjing ● Shanghai ●
SHANGHAI

HUBEI

Wuhan ●

N

CHONGQING

Yangtze

ZHEJIANG

East
China
Sea

HUNAN

JIANGXI

GUIZHOU

FUJIAN

Taipei ●

Tropic of Cancer

GUANGXI ZHUANG
AUTONOMOUS
REGION

GUANGDONG

Pearl

River

Guangzhou ●

TAIWAN

Hong Kong

HONG KONG SPECIAL
ADMINISTRATIVE REGION

MACAU SPECIAL
ADMINISTRATIVE REGION

PACIFIC OCEAN

VIETNAM

HAINAN

Gulf of
Tonkin

South
China
Sea

PHILIPPINES

0   180   360   540 miles

Scale

CHINA
Land, Life, and Culture

Arts and Culture

JOHN AND JACKIE TIDEY

Marshall Cavendish
Benchmark
New York

This edition first published in 2009 in the United States of America by Marshall Cavendish Benchmark.

Marshall Cavendish Benchmark
99 White Plains Road
Tarrytown, NY 10591
www.marshallcavendish.us

All Internet sites were available and accurate when sent to press.

First published in 2008 by
MACMILLAN EDUCATION AUSTRALIA PTY LTD
15–19 Claremont Street, South Yarra 3141

Visit our website at www.macmillan.com.au or go directly to www.macmillanlibrary.com.au

Associated companies and representatives throughout the world.

Copyright © John and Jackie Tidey 2008

Library of Congress Cataloging-in-Publication Data

Tidey, John.
    Arts and culture / by John and Jackie Tidey.
        p. cm. — (China—land, life, and culture)
    Includes index.
    ISBN 978-0-7614-3154-1
    1. Arts, Chinese—Juvenile literature. I. Tidey, Jackie. II. Title.
    NX583.A1T53 2008
    700.951—dc22
                                                    2008002848

Edited by Georgina Garner
Text and cover design by Peter Shaw
Page layout by Peter Shaw
Photo research by Jes Senbergs
Maps by Damien Demaj, DEMAP

Printed in the United States

Acknowledgments
The author and the publisher are grateful to the following for permission to reproduce copyright material:

Cover photograph: dragon at Chinese New Year Festival, by © Stucorlett/Dreamstime.com

Aquarius Collection/Interfilm, 23 (bottom); Leo Carol – wildmind.com.au; Michelle Clarke, 5 (top), 24 (bottom); Corbis, 25; © Elenaray/Dreamstime.com, 8 (top); © H3ct02/Dreamstime.com, 11 (top); © Stucorlett/Dreamstime.com, 1, 10; Marion Ducco, 3 (top right), 4 (top right), 6 (bottom), 18, 19 (top); Fotosearch, 20 (bottom); Getty Images, 6 (top), 9, 11 (bottom), 13 (top & bottom), 15, 17, 21, 22, 23 (top), 30 (top & left); China Photos/Getty Images, 28; © istockphoto.com, 4 (bottom left); © Ying Chen/istockphoto, 4 (bottom right) © Jin Young Lee/istockphoto 24 (top); © Hector Joseph Lumang/istockphoto, 14 (top left); Mike and Jane Pelusey, 16 (top); © Thomas Barret/Shutterstock, 26; © Zhu Difeng/Shutterstock, 3 (bottom left), 20 (top); © Max FX/Shutterstock, 4 (bottom middle); © Stelian Ion/Shutterstock, 14 (middle); © Pieter Janssen/Shutterstock, 5 (bottom); © Sharon Kennedy/Shutterstock, 14 (top right); © Timur Kulgarin/Shutterstock, 7; © Taol Mor/Shutterstock, 14 (bottom right), 24 (middle); © CHEN WE1 SENG Shutterstock, 29 (top); © Ke Wang/Shutterstock, 14 (bottom left); Jackie Tidey 8 (bottom); Wikimedia Commons, Dr. Meierhofer, 29 (bottom); James Wu, 3 (top left), 4 (top left & top middle), 12, 16 (bottom), 19 (bottom), 27, 30 (right).

While every care has been taken to trace and acknowledge copyright, the publisher tenders their apologies for any accidental infringement where copyright has proved untraceable. Where the attempt has been unsuccessful, the publisher welcomes information that would redress the situation.

1 3 5 6 4 2

Contents

Glossary Words

When a word is printed in **bold**, you can look up its meaning in the Glossary on page 31.

Chinese Proverb

With time and patience, the mulberry leaf becomes a silk gown.

China, A Big Country

China challenges the imagination because of its size. It is big in many ways. It is one of the largest countries on Earth, covering about one-fifth of the continent of Asia. China's population of more than 1.3 billion, or 1,300,000,000, is the world's largest. It has an ancient civilization and a recorded history that date back thousands of years.

A large area of China is covered by tall mountains and wide deserts. Most of the population lives in the fertile lowlands that are bordered by the Pacific Ocean in the east.

The People's Republic of China

Today, China is formally known as the People's Republic of China (P.R.C.). In the last thirty years, the PRC have gone through great social change and the **economy** has grown enormously. China is now one of the United States' major trading partners.

This book explores the rich art and culture that has emerged over thousands of years in China's ancient, complex, and fascinating society.

An ancient history

Traditional arts

Very old customs

A country of extremes

A rich variety of wildlife

Plants and medicinal herbs

Chinese Culture

China's unique and inspiring culture dates back more than five thousand years. Culture has been described as the way of life for a whole society. It covers a wide range of things, from art and beliefs to music, literature, dress, and customs.

Traditions

Chinese culture has many traditions. Calligraphy and chop engraving are treasured skills from ancient times that are still in use today. **Fables** have enriched Chinese storytelling for thousands of years, and some of these are still read and retold today. There are many objects and ideas that have shaped life in China. Chinese opera, music, pottery, dance, and puppetry are all traditions that are still valued today.

The lion statues found in front of Chinese palaces are thought to act as guardians.

Chinese opera is a combination of music, dance, drama, and acrobatics.

Did You Know?

The abacus is a mechanical aid for counting. It has been used in China for well over two thousand years, and it is still in use today.

Calligraphy

The word calligraphy means "beautiful writing." It is an art that dates back thousands of years, and it is still widely practiced throughout China.

Writing As an Art Form

Calligraphy has long been regarded as China's highest form of visual art. It began in China about 3,500 years ago with the development of a complex writing system that uses more than 1,500 characters.

Calligraphy is much more than a system of beautiful writing. It is regarded as an art form in China. Examples of calligraphy are displayed in galleries and museums in the same way that paintings are displayed.

Chinese children learn the art of calligraphy from an early age.

For Your Information

There are three main styles of calligraphy in the world:

- Western
- Arabic
- Chinese

Did You Know?

The origins of calligraphy can be traced back to cave paintings in Egypt more than five thousand years ago.

Chinese galleries display works of calligraphy by different artists.

Early Writing and Paper

Some of the earliest examples of Chinese writing are **inscriptions** found on animal bones and tortoise shells, dating from around 1400 BCE. Much later, but still well before the invention of the modern printing press in 1490 CE, books were individually handwritten and copied by a **scribe**.

Writing has been around for a very long time, but paper to write on did not always exist. Before paper, people wrote on all sorts of things, such as wood, cloth, and the papyrus plant. Paper made from bark pulp was invented in China about two thousand years ago.

Calligraphy as Self-Expression

The practice of calligraphy is also a method of self-expression. It is said that calligraphy can be thought of as a silent reflection of the soul or as a mirror of our inner selves.

For Your Information

The tools used for centuries by Chinese calligraphers are sometimes called the Four Treasures of the Study. These four treasures are:

- the writing brush, which may be made with the hair of the yellow weasel or, sometimes, the black rabbit
- the ink stick, which is a solid bar of special pigment that is used to make the ink
- the inkstone, which holds the liquid ink and is made from stone or pottery
- the paper

A calligrapher practices his art with complete concentration.

Chops

A chop is a personal stamp or seal. The chop has been used in China for more than three thousand years. It still plays a very important part in the business and artistic life of China.

Name Chops

After signing their name on a document, it is necessary for someone to stamp it with their chop before it is legally binding. Often a personal name chop is a work of art, with beautiful engravings.

Artists stamp their works with their name chop, too. This is for two reasons. It is proof that the piece of work is **authentic**, and it is also the way artists sign their work. In fact, traditional paintings and calligraphy are not complete unless they are stamped with the artist's chop.

Company Chops

A company has to get a chop before it operates in China. All company chops are registered with a government office, and there is just one per company. Signatures do not count in Chinese business. Documents must be chopped.

Chops may be decorated with different carvings.

personal chop

ink paste

stamp

A personal chop and ink paste is used to stamp a name.

8

Chop Engraving

Chop engraving, calligraphy, and painting are the three great visual arts in China. They are thought of as treasures of Chinese civilization. After thousands of years, the art of chop carving is still highly respected and honored. There is usually a special category for chops in fine art exhibitions.

Chops were traditionally engraved by hand in copper or jade. A wide range of styles is available today. Wood, stone, and various metal alloys, or combinations, may be used.

Chops are engraved by skilled artists.

Ink Paste

After it has been engraved, the chop is pressed into a red ink paste and stamped onto a surface, usually paper. This is when the piece of art becomes an item of practical use. A good ink paste has a brilliant, rich, red color, because it needs to keep its original beauty and function for a very long time.

Did You Know?

The bright red color in ink paste comes from cinnabar, a mineral found in Hunan Province in China and in other parts of the world.

Festivals

Chinese festivals are colorful events, full of old traditions. They often involve special foods, family, drums, loud music, fireworks, lanterns, and other decorations.

Chinese New Year

Chinese New Year falls on a different day each year, but always around late January or February. It happens at the same time as the first new moon of the year, and it is the most important festival in the Chinese year.

For weeks before New Year, houses are cleaned and decorated with lanterns or paper cutouts in red and gold, the Chinese colors of good fortune or luck. People travel to be with their families. A reunion meal is planned for the evening before the big day, usually away from home at a restaurant. Small red envelopes containing money are given as New Year gifts. Often, there are processions in the streets and fireworks displays.

Did You Know?

People clean their houses before the Chinese New Year. It is considered unlucky to do this at New Year because you might sweep the good luck from your house.

At Chinese New Year, many people hide under the drapes of a Chinese dragon and twist and turn it through the streets in a dragon dance.

Mid-Autumn Festival

Families gather outside to eat mooncakes and look at the full moon together during the Mid-Autumn Festival. This festival occurs in September or October. After dark, children walk around carrying lanterns with candles inside them.

National Day

China's National Day is celebrated on the first of October. It celebrates the founding of the People's Republic of China in 1949. The declaration of the new China was made in Tiananmen Square, so each year special decorations and flower displays cover the square to mark the event.

Flag raising ceremonies occur all over China and the national anthem is played. Crowds watch the flag raising ceremonies and wave flags to celebrate. National Day is the beginning of a weeklong holiday. Chinese people use the opportunity of this holiday to travel all over the country.

At night in Hong Kong and Shanghai, huge firework displays mark National Day over Hong Kong's harbor and along Shanghai's Huangpu River.

Mooncakes are filled with sweet bean paste.

Did You Know?

The national anthem of China is called "The March of the Volunteers."

The fireworks over Tiananmen Square on National Day are watched by huge crowds.

Porcelain

Porcelain is sometimes called "fine china." It is a **ceramic** material that is used to make objects such as vases, cups, bowls, and boxes. Because of its **durability** and attractiveness, porcelain objects became a part of daily life in China, particularly for the wealthier classes of people. Porcelain was one of the early types of artwork that was taken to the **Western** world along the famous **Silk Road**.

The term porcelain covers a wide range of ceramic products that have been baked at very high temperatures of about 2100 degrees Fahrenheit (1150 degrees Celsius). Some of the earliest porcelain, made in China more than 3,500 years ago, was made of kaolin, which is a fine, white clay.

Modern Porcelain

Thousands of years after it was first made, the making of porcelain is still a popular art with collectors and admirers around the world. How it is made has partly changed, but the basic features of porcelain remain the same, such as style, texture, elegance, and decoration.

Did You Know?

Porcelain objects from different times in history have been found in shipwrecks. Wrecks that settled on the seabed hundreds of years ago can act as time capsules.

This porcelain vase was made about 250 years ago, during the Qing Dynasty.

Jingdezhen Porcelain

For those who collect or study Chinese antiques, the ancient town of Jingdezhen is a special place. Jingdezhen, in the remote Jiangxi Province, was once the porcelain capital of China. Its ceramics are famous as a symbol of Chinese and Eastern art. More than one thousand years ago, beautiful porcelain objects produced in the kilns and workshops of Jingdezhen covered the tables and living rooms of China's emperors.

Jingdezhen was closed to foreigners for many years, as was the rest of China. The skills and secrets of Jingdezhen's porcelain makers are now shared with the world, and visitors are very welcome. The craft was in decline, but today it is undergoing a very big revival.

Jingdezhen is a town in the northeast of Jiangxi Province.

Porcelain vases are lined up outside a workshop in Jingdezhen.

A worker makes a large jar at a porcelain workshop in Jingdezhen.

Did You Know?

Porcelain is used to make decorative objects, and it is also used in dentistry to make false teeth and crowns.

Yin and Yang

Yin and *yang* is an ancient Chinese concept. To a Westerner's mind, *yin* and *yang* might seem mysterious. *Yin* and *yang* represent the two opposite sides of nature. *Yin* is the darker element. It is passive, feminine, dark, and corresponds to the night. *Yang* is seen as brighter. It is masculine and corresponds to day. Often, *yin* is symbolized by earth or water and *yang* by wind or fire.

The Yin and Yang Symbol

The Chinese *yin* and *yang* symbol is also known as the Tai Chi Symbol. It represents a kind of balance of opposites. When *yin* and *yang* are equally present, everything is calm. If one is overwhelmed by the other, then there is confusion, not calm.

Fire

Water

Yin and Yang symbol

Earth

Wind

14

The Concept of Yin and Yang

The concept of *yin* and *yang* has been traced back more than three thousand years. For more than two thousand years, the principles of *yin* and *yang* have been an important part of traditional Chinese medicine. This concept of balance is also one of the basic theories behind the tradition of *feng shui*.

Those who study *yin* and *yang* believe that this concept applies to everything. It is believed that while *yin* and *yang* are opposites in nature, they are also part of nature, they rely on each other and cannot exist without each other, and if one is stronger then the other will be weaker.

Did You Know?

In ancient times, Chinese people thought thunder and lightning were a clash of *yin* and *yang*.

Lightning crashes over the city of Guangzhou, in Guangdong Province.

Music

Music is a very important part of Chinese people's lives. It is quite common in public places all over China to see small groups of musicians playing together on traditional instruments. There is always music playing at family celebrations.

Records of a well-developed musical culture date back about 2,500 years. When Western music was just beginning, Chinese people had already developed complex musical instruments quite different in tone and appearance to those now seen in a Western orchestra.

Street musicians are a common sight in China's big cities.

For Your Information

Traditional Chinese music has a five note tonal scale. The five notes can be given the names *gong*, *shang*, *jiao*, *zi*, and *yu*. Western music has an eight note scale. These eight notes can be given the names *do*, *re*, *mi*, *fa*, *so*, *la*, *ti*, and *do*. The different tonal scales of Chinese and Western music make for a big difference in the sound of the music.

This large Chinese instrument is called a *gu zheng*, and the smaller instrument is a *pipa*.

Instruments

There are big differences between the sound of Chinese music and the sound of Western music. Most of these differences come from the Chinese musical instruments themselves, which are unique to the region. Like Western instruments, such as the flute, violin, cello, and drums, Chinese musical instruments can be divided into four basic types: they can be blown, bowed, plucked, or banged.

Chinese instruments come in different shapes and sizes, such as:
- the *er-hu*, which is a two-stringed fiddle
- the *gu zheng*, which is an instrument with somewhere between sixteen and twenty-five strings
- the *pipa*, which is a grand, four-stringed lute
- the *dadi*, which is a flute

Changing Musical Tastes

Young people in China listen to a lot of Western bands, such as Coldplay, Queen, and Nirvana. They also have their own pop stars, such as Faye Wong, who is Chinese music's megastar. Wong is also famous because of another branch of the entertainment industry, video games. Her song "Eyes on Me" was recorded for the video game *Final Fantasy VIII*.

One of the problems with being a pop star in China is that it is hard to make any money from CD sales, because **piracy** is very common.

Faye Wong is a popular singer from Hong Kong.

Did You Know?

There are very few live music venues for pop music in China's big cities. However, karaoke is everywhere and is very popular with young Chinese.

For Your Information

Gulangyu, near the seaport city of Xiamen, in Fujian Province, is also known as Piano Island. Its population of about 18,000 people love music and own more than six hundred pianos. This island is home to a piano museum.

Chinese Opera

This popular form of drama with music, mime, dancing, and acrobatics began during the Tang Dynasty, which ruled from 618 CE until 907 CE. When opera began in China, the opera **troupes** performed mainly for the emperor's pleasure. Since then, opera has become an art form for the people and it has developed into many different forms and styles. It has become a regional art with local traditions and stories.

In the big cities, such as Beijing, opera is quite a **sophisticated** entertainment. In other regions, it can involve funny scenes, loud voices, and acrobatics. Two important elements that are central to all Chinese opera performances are the costumes and the masks or face paint. These are always brightly colored to help the audience work out which character is which.

For Your Information

The color of the face paint on each character helps the audience to figure out what kind of character is on stage:

- a red face is for a brave, loyal person
- a white face shows treachery
- a green face is bad-tempered and surly

The costumes and makeup in Chinese opera are very detailed.

Opera Singers

The peak of success for an opera singer in China is to join an opera troupe in a big city and perform Beijing opera. In a country with so many people and where opera is so popular, a person has to be very determined and focused to become a Beijing opera singer. It is a long journey from a country village to a local drama and opera school, but if someone shows promise, they may be lucky enough to go to the China Academy of Traditional Opera in Beijing.

An opera singer applies his face makeup before a performance.

Did You Know?

Mei Lanfang (1894–1961) was a very famous Beijing opera performer. He played mainly female, or *dan*, roles and his fame spread all over China and the world. Today, female roles are played by women.

MEET Wu Shaomei

Wu Shaomei is from a small village in Shanxi Province. Her ambition is to be an opera singer in the Beijing opera.

In Conversation with Wu Shaomei

At the moment, I am singing with my local opera and training with a local opera school. I want to go to the China Academy in Beijing because it is the best place to train to be an opera singer. My teacher thinks I will be ready to take the test next year.

In the meantime, I try to get as many parts in my local opera as I can because it is good experience.

Literature

China's literature goes back at least three thousand years to a time before paper was invented. Early literature often gave advice about how people should behave and how society should be organized. Confucius (551 BCE–479 BCE) and Lao-tzu (about 600 BCE or 400 BCE) are probably the best known of the early writers of philosophy and religion.

One Language

The Chinese written language uses characters that are like little pictures, called pictographs. The characters stand for things or ideas, rather than the way Western letters of the alphabet stand for sounds.

The written language all over China can be read by everyone who understands enough of the written characters. It does not change between locally spoken **dialects**. If people from different regions of China who speak different dialects wrote down what they were saying, it would look the same and have the same characters.

This written language is shared by all Chinese people. A common written language has helped develop common, continuous cultural traditions for millions of Chinese people.

The wise sayings of Confucius are popular in both China and the West.

The writings of Lao-tzu are thought to have started the philosophy of Taoism.

Poetry and History

All forms of the written word in China date back thousands of years. Poetry was an early art form that has always been popular. Classical poems from the Tang Dynasty poet Li Po (700 CE–762 CE) are still read today. Historical writing was an early form of writing, also. Often, the rulers of a dynasty would order a history of the previous dynasty to be written by the scholars of the day.

Novels and Fables

Early novels were adventures or tales of the supernatural. Historical stories and love stories were also popular. Some fables have survived through the centuries and are read and retold still.

For Your Information

During the Qin Dynasty (221 BCE until 207 BCE), all the lands of China were unified for the first time under one emperor, Qin Shi Huangdi. Qin Shi Huangdi wanted the books that offered advice for correct living and governing to be destroyed, and so he ordered the books to be burned. The dynasty that came after him had to reconstruct the texts of the **Classics** from books that survived the burning.

Cultural Revolution

About one hundred years ago, China was plunged into **turmoil** when the last dynasty was overthrown. A lot of Chinese writing from this time focuses on the troubles the country went through as it struggled to discard old ways of living. During Mao Zedong's Cultural Revolution of 1966 to 1976, all cultural traditions from the past were discarded. Since the late 1970s, a new generation of writers has emerged and is being encouraged to record the changes Chinese people are experiencing.

Huge posters encouraged people to speak out against those who did not share Mao Zedong's ideals.

Movies

China has been making movies since the early 1900s. At first, Chinese movies were short movies or movies of stage plays, which were mainly made for local viewers. In 1910, China's first movie studio opened. Chinese moviemaking then went through many stages, depending on the political situation in the country at the time. At times it was a thriving industry making popular movies that won international awards. At other times, because of censorship and government pressure, the movies that were made were more or less **propaganda** movies.

New Movies

In 1976, after the death of Mao Zedong, the movie industry gradually began to make new movies. In 1985, the movie *Yellow Earth* won awards and drew attention to the work of Chinese moviemakers. Since then, Chinese movies have become very popular with moviegoers around the world.

The stories that Chinese movies tell are nearly always stories of ordinary people and life in China, or stories from Chinese history. Because so little was known about China, these movies often enjoyed great success in the West. Many Chinese movie actors now star in Hollywood movies and Chinese movie directors work in Hollywood, too.

The Chinese actor Bruce Lee appeared in many U.S. movies, including the most famous *kung fu* movie ever made, *Enter the Dragon*.

MEET Zhang Yimou

Zhang Yimou is a world-famous movie director who lives and works in the People's Republic of China. He has made many movies about life in China that have won awards and are well known around the world.

In Conversation with Zhang Yimou

Most of my movies are stories from Chinese history. We have such a long history and so many stories that I am never going to run out of ideas for movies.

My recent movie *Hero* is about the First Emperor of a united China. It is set in the Qin Dynasty. That emperor was the one who ordered the Great Wall to be built. It is a martial arts movie but it is also a beautiful movie, not just an action movie.

In China, the visual poetry is very important. I wanted to put the art back into martial arts.

Did You Know?

Other Chinese movies that are very popular are the *kung fu* films that starred Bruce Lee, which were made in Hong Kong.

Zhang Yimou's movie *Hero* was very successful, both in China and around the world.

23

Painting

The earliest Chinese paintings that have been found date back to at least 200 BCE. Chinese paintings have a traditional subject matter and form.

Subject Matter

The subject matter of Chinese paintings is usually nature, birds, and flowers. The earliest paintings were of small and delicate birds and flowers. From about 1000 CE onward, landscape *shanshui* painting with mountains and streams became the most important aspect of Chinese art. This was considered a substitute for nature, because it allowed viewers to wander in their imaginations through beautiful landscapes.

Brushwork

In Chinese painting, brushwork is very important. In this way, painting is very close to calligraphy, which the Chinese consider the highest form of artistic expression.

Traditional Chinese artists believe that brushwork brings out the rhythm, life, and vitality in a painting. Although they might look at examples of brushwork from the great Chinese artists, painters try to develop their own style.

Early paintings were of birds and flowers.

Shanshui paintings are of landscape scenes.

A Chinese artist may work with inks and watercolors.

24

Composition

How all the pieces are positioned in a painting is also very important. The *yin* and *yang* balance, which is so important to Chinese people, is something that is present in great examples of Chinese art.

Blank Space in Paintings

Chinese artists always leave a large blank space in their paintings. This is deliberate. In bird and flower paintings, this represents the sky. In *shanshui* paintings, it represents the sky, clouds, mist, and water.

A blank space is an important part of a Chinese painting. Leaving part of the painting untouched allows the viewer to fill in the scenery with their imagination or feelings.

Inscriptions and Seals

Inscriptions and seals are often found in the empty spaces of a painting. They add beauty to the work. Sometimes the inscription is written in beautiful calligraphy by a different artist or poet. The seal is nearly always red in color. Sometimes, it is the artist's name, and sometimes, it is just decoration.

Did You Know?

Some Chinese artists believe that they cannot become an outstanding traditional painter until they have mastered the art of calligraphy.

This painting has blank space and an inscription written in calligraphy.

Martial Arts

The Chinese martial arts are forms of unarmed self-defense. There are many martial art styles in China, and some of these can be traced back more than three thousand years. They began because of military, hunting, and self-defense needs and, over time, they became an important part of Chinese culture. To most Westerners, Chinese martial arts are known as *kung fu* or *wushu*.

Correct Wushu Training

Wushu means "martial methods." Correct *wushu* training improves health, fitness, and determination. It is thought to give a student skills in a competitive sport, a way to defend themselves, and a personal art form.

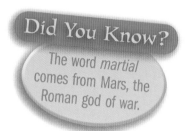

Did You Know?
The word *martial* comes from Mars, the Roman god of war.

Kung fu Books and Movies

Martial arts novels were written in China during the Ming Dynasty and are still written today. Martial arts movies are also very popular. Two very famous ones are *Enter the Dragon* (1973) and *Crouching Tiger, Hidden Dragon* (1999). Martial arts films are often called *kung fu* films.

People practice the martial art of tai chi for physical and mental health.

Kites

Kites in China have a long history, perhaps dating back as long as three thousand years ago. Early kites were made of wood and were used for military purposes, although how they were used is unclear. There are many tales about a Chinese general who tied a young soldier to a kite and flew him over an enemy camp to spy on an enemy.

Kites for Pleasure

In time, kites began to be used for pleasure. Bamboo and silk were used to make them. The combination of these two materials is still used to make the best Chinese kites. Although these materials sound fragile, they are stronger than steel and much more durable.

Kites as Art

Chinese kites are works of art. They come in an endless assortment of shapes and styles. Some of them are as small as the palm of an adult's hand, and others are as big as a small airplane.

The art that decorates most Chinese kites has a symbolic meaning or illustrates a character or emblem from Chinese folklore or history. Tortoises, cranes, and peaches mean long life, bats are a sign of good luck, butterflies and flowers represent harmony, and a dragon represents power and prosperity.

Did You Know?

Weifang, a city in Shandong Province, is famous for its kite-building and has a huge kite festival each year. Weifang also has a kite museum.

This kite seller in Shanghai offers a selection of Chinese kites.

Puppetry

Puppetry in China dates back to ancient times. It has an important place in folk celebrations and religious ceremonies. Puppetry comes in several forms:

- the marionette theater
- the glove theater
- the shadow theater

String Puppets

A marionette, or string puppet, is moved from above using strings or threads attached to its head, arms, and legs. The more strings that are used on a puppet, the more control there is over its movements.

Traditional marionette theater brings together language, history, religion, and music. It is still very popular today.

For Your Information

Puppetry in China is not just an amusement for children or a bit of fun. It is considered a great art. Puppetry has influenced the development of other forms of Chinese theater.

A man operates a Chinese marionette with many strings.

Glove Puppets

Chinese glove, or hand, puppets are usually about 8 inches (20 centimeters) long. They are operated by a person, who places one hand inside the puppet. Some are made of wood and others of papier-mache or plastic. These puppets come in a great variety of characters. Traditional Chinese historical novels have been cleverly adapted for the glove puppet theater.

Shadow Puppets

China is sometimes called "the home of shadow play." This form of puppetry has been practiced widely in China for more than two thousand years. Shadow puppets are painted or stained in many colors. They may be made from leather, cardboard, metal, theatrical gels, or plastic. Shadow play is a two-dimensional activity. It requires highly skilled techniques in performance. As well as being used in performances, shadow puppets are also treasured as a kind of artwork.

One hand is placed inside the glove puppet and the other is used to move different parts of the puppet.

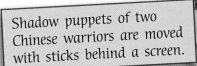
Shadow puppets of two Chinese warriors are moved with sticks behind a screen.

Moving with the Times

Modern China protects and celebrates its ancient art and culture, but it also moves with the times. Chinese movies are popular with audiences around the world. Paintings done by modern Chinese artists make large sums at auctions in major international cities. Touring companies of acrobats, dancers, and musicians show the world new ways to perform traditional art forms. The world is increasingly fascinated by all things Chinese.

China went through turmoil during the Cultural Revolution of 1966 to 1976. For much of that time, its schools and colleges were shut and students were encouraged to challenge and **persecute** teachers, artists, and intellectuals.

Since the Cultural Revolution, China has gone through another period of change. Contact with the West and increasing wealth has seen a new flowering of all artistic forms. Chinese artists are conscious of their traditional heritage but they embrace elements of Western influence in their work. The **fusion** of East and West in art is just beginning.

Musicians in modern Chinese bands may use Western instruments.

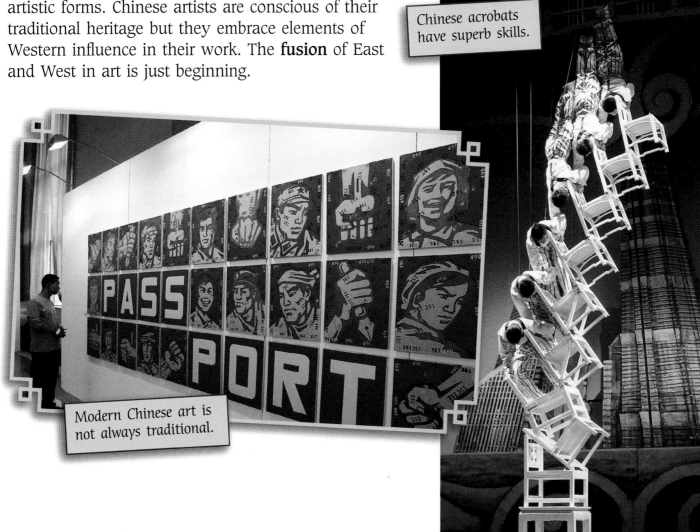

Chinese acrobats have superb skills.

Modern Chinese art is not always traditional.

Glossary

authentic	real or genuine
ceramic	made from clay and similar materials
Classics	the famous *Four Books* in Chinese literature, *Daxue*, *Zhongyong*, *Mengzi,* and *Lunyu*, which were studied in all schools
dialects	different spoken forms of a language
durability	the quality of lasting or not wearing out
economy	the finances of a country
fables	made-up stories that teach lessons about how to behave
fusion	the blending of different things into one
inscriptions	brief written or stamped dedications in a book or on a piece of art
persecute	to mistreat someone because of religious or political beliefs
piracy	the copying of copyrighted work, such as music, without permission
propaganda	information that is used to try to make someone believe a certain point of view
scribe	someone who makes copies of written manuscripts
Silk Road	famous series of trade routes in ancient China
sophisticated	worldly wise from education or experience
troupes	groups of entertainers
turmoil	a state of commotion, disorder, or disturbance
Western	related to the parts of the developed world that are not covered by eastern Asia

Index

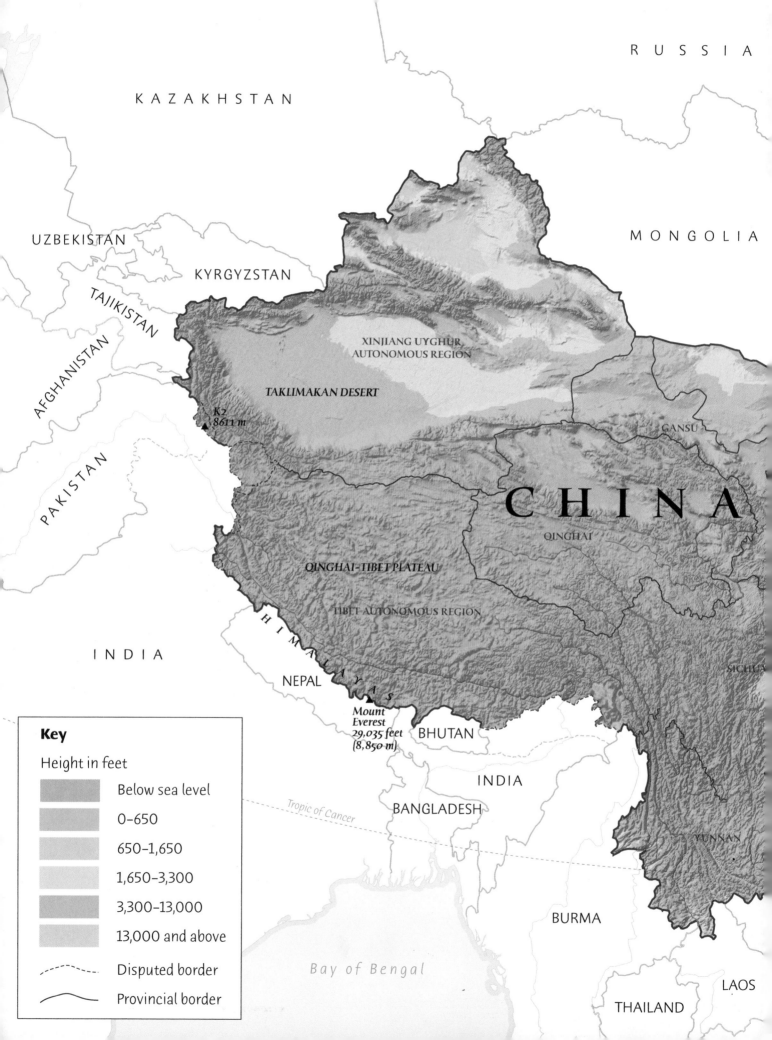

RUSSIA

KAZAKHSTAN

UZBEKISTAN

KYRGYZSTAN

MONGOLIA

TAJIKISTAN

AFGHANISTAN

XINJIANG UYGHUR
AUTONOMOUS REGION

TAKLIMAKAN DESERT

GANSU

PAKISTAN

K2
8611 m

CHINA

QINGHAI

QINGHAI-TIBET PLATEAU

TIBET AUTONOMOUS REGION

SICHUA

INDIA

H I M A L A Y A S

NEPAL

Mount
Everest
29,035 feet
(8,850 m)

BHUTAN

INDIA

BANGLADESH

Tropic of Cancer

YUNNAN

Key

Height in feet

Below sea level

0–650

650–1,650

1,650–3,300

3,300–13,000

13,000 and above

- - - - Disputed border

——— Provincial border

BURMA

Bay of Bengal

LAOS

THAILAND